To Gene Moore

Phil 4:6-7

Blessings
        Mark Randall

The Bethlehem Midwife

*The Story of Jesus' Birth, Retold through
the Eyes of a Midwife*

MARK RANDALL, M.D.

CROSSBOOKS
PUBLISHING

CrossBooks™
A Division of LifeWay
1663 Liberty Drive
Bloomington, IN 47403
www.crossbooks.com
Phone: 1-866-879-0502

First published by CrossBooks 9/30/2013

ISBN: 978-1-4627-3207-4 (sc)
ISBN: 978-1-4627-3208-1 (e)

Library of Congress Control Number: 2013917566

Printed in the United States of America.

This book is printed on acid-free paper.

Table of Contents

For my mother, Shirley Irene Jackson Randall

A voice is heard in Ramah,
mourning and great weeping
Rachel weeping for her children
and refusing to be comforted,
because her children are no more.

This is what the Lord says:
"Restrain your voice from weeping
and your eyes from tears,
for your work will be rewarded."
—Jeremiah 31:15–16a (NIV)[1]

Preface

When my wife and I were expecting our first child, we made a major move. I left my practice in Alabama to go to seminary in Texas. We were nervous as we loaded up all our belongings into two cars and drove to a strange city where we didn't know anyone. Shortly after our arrival there, our four-pound son, Miles, arrived prematurely on December 23. Even though he was the smallest child in the nursery, we were given permission to take Miles home two days later on Christmas Day because I was a doctor. We had to place him in a shoe box temporarily; we didn't have a crib yet because of his early arrival. Since there was nowhere for him to sleep, we pulled out a sock drawer, padded it, and laid him in it. He slept in this drawer for the next couple of days until we could buy a crib.

This experience led me to consider what it might have been like for Mary and Joseph to arrive in a strange village without any friends or family. What was it like for Mary to deliver her son in Bethlehem? How did she improvise a crib? Did she have anyone to help her? There were no doctors or nurses back then, but were there midwives in those days who could have helped her? Is it possible that Mary received a midwife's assistance during the birth? As I consulted the Bible for answers, I noticed that since the earliest of times, midwives had helped Jewish women deliver their babies. In Genesis 28:27-30, a midwife helped Tamar deliver her twins and tied a scarlet thread on her son. Again, in Exodus 1:15-20, Shiphrah and Puah were midwives in Egypt who saved the Israelite baby boys from Pharaoh. Based on this, I thought it was highly likely that there were midwives in every town of Palestine who helped young ladies deliver their babies. This caused me to wonder if there was a midwife in Bethlehem that night, and if so, how she would have interacted with Mary and Joseph, the shepherds, and later the wise men.

This story is a summary of the Christmas story as seen through the eyes of a midwife and her husband. I have lived overseas for many years and have delivered babies in Thailand and Zimbabwe as well as in the United States. In each country, I have seen and appreciated the work of midwives. I have based this fictitious story on the second chapters of both Matthew and Luke and on my observations of midwives at work. I have tried to describe the delivery as realistically as possible, as this helps me to appreciate the suffering and the unhygienic conditions Mary was willing to endure because of her faith in God. For Mary to be willing to leave her home, loving family, and friends to deliver her son in an unknown city just because she was called to do so is amazing. I am overwhelmed that God loved us so much that he was willing to stoop so low as to send his Son to be born in a dirty stable. This is a stark contrast to the typical pastoral manger scene one usually thinks of where Mary, Joseph, and baby Jesus are surrounded by peaceful animals with accompanying shepherds and wise men. I wanted to show not only the physical suffering of Mary going through childbirth but also the psychological suffering she endured from the stigma of being pregnant prior to her wedding and her isolation in a strange city away from family and friends who would have helped. I do believe there would have been some community involvement in Bethlehem to help Mary through this traumatic time.

In July 2013, my hospital had to be evacuated in twenty minutes because of a bomb threat. It was difficult pushing the patients out in beds, wheelchairs, and office chairs, but the community quickly helped. The local funeral home had a tent set up in twenty minutes to shield the ambulatory patients from the rain. Walmart sent four tents, and a local church sent their bus to add to the twelve ambulances ferrying the sickest patients to other hospitals and shelters. As I was triaging patients, someone told me one patient was in labor. I saw a group of ten strangers holding up sheets and umbrellas around a bed parked under an oak tree. I was thankful to find that the lady's OB doctor was already there coaxing her through the delivery. I assisted by locating needed items, like a bag of saline and a flashlight, from the paramedics. It was a relief to hear the baby's first cry when she finally arrived, and many of us in the parking lot clapped and cheered. I think Bethlehem would have come to the assistance of Mary and Joseph and called the lady who delivered babies to help them. The people of Bethlehem showed incredible loyalty and sacrifice not to betray to Herod's soldiers the baby's location in spite of the loss of their own children.

I also wanted to spotlight Joseph's character of obedience. Four times in the Gospels, it says that Joseph received instructions in a dream, starting with taking pregnant Mary to be his wife. Every time, he obeyed immediately. When God looked for an earthly father to raise his Son, he chose a man who modeled instant obedience so that when God the Father asked his Son to die on the cross, Jesus responded, "Not my will but thine."

I tried to describe the birth as medically accurately as possible. Three midwives proofed the description and made good suggestions. All of them pointed out that they had been trained "not to push on the abdomen," as this could injure the baby and would only be used as a measure of last resort if they couldn't get to a hospital. I understand that today, this is the standard of care, but I have seen several midwives use this technique in Africa and Asia and speculate that this may have been a logical thing for a midwife to do two thousand years ago. Women in Palestine were using salt at deliveries as recently as one hundred years ago. It is uncertain when this custom started. Due to its antiseptic qualities, it is a much better solution than the grass and manure poultices I have seen on newborns' umbilical stumps, which can cause tetanus.

The reason I had the wise men arrive in Bethlehem when Jesus was a toddler was the Gospels mention they came to a "house," not a stable, to a young child, not a baby, and they had told Herod the star appeared two years earlier. Although I have tried to be as realistic as possible, others have criticized me for having three wise men when the Bible does not give the number but only three gifts. I have decided to go with three wise men based on my experience living in an Eastern culture. There, whenever someone came to my house, he or she brought a gift—tea, fruit, alcohol, candy, or dried rabbit and almost always from his or her hometown, giving a part of him- or herself. No one ever came without a personal gift, so I think each gift would represent one person bearing a gift from his home region, such as the myrrh and frankincense. From the time of Jesus' birth to the wise men's arrival, I feel sure that the family stayed in Bethlehem and that Joseph would have worked at his profession to provide his family with food. It probably required a trip back to Nazareth to reclaim his bulky tools. During those times, a man usually learned the same trade as his father, and most likely, his tools would have been handed down. The olive press is based on the one I saw at the museum in seminary.

There are inaccuracies in this story, as I have not lived in the Middle East, and there are also errors due to this being my first book. These are my mistakes, but I hope you will overlook them and instead let this story stimulate you to look at Christmas in a different light. May this book give you a fresh perspective in appreciating the difficulties Mary and Joseph experienced in welcoming our Savior. Above all, I want you to know that Jesus loves you so much that he was willing to humble himself to come to earth to rescue you.

Acknowledgments

I love and appreciate my wife, Tina Marsalete Westerfield, who has been so faithful to have and raise our children in faraway cities and other countries.

I am also grateful to Margaret Dunaway, who started the midwifery school at Sanyati Baptist Hospital, Zimbabwe. I am sure she found my friend Chip and me very annoying as children, always coming to the hospital to get plastic syringes for water pistols and peering in the window of labor and delivery. Eventually, she put up curtains to keep us from looking in. Thank you to Martha Dunaway Weaver, her daughter, for her comments. She follows in her mother's footsteps as a midwife. Thank you, Ann Burfitt, Janet Erwin, Kim Davis, and Sue Salstrand, for your good suggestions and midwifery advice. Thank you for your photos of hands, Evie, Bob, Marilyn, and Jim, which bring the story to life.

Ray Crump, it was good to meet you at my son's baseball game and to learn about your work with the Committee on Relief. I was fascinated to learn that for eight dollars, you can package a birthing kit containing two flannel blankets, a polypropylene sheet, three sutures, a blade, soap, and gloves. This is in accordance with the WHO recommendations, and it has been found to reduce infant mortality rates by 80 percent when used in third-world countries. It is great that you were able to send out 1,200 kits last year. I appreciate your being willing to use all proceeds from this book to purchase more midwifery kits to send out. To learn more about this outreach, please go to:

www.umdisasterwarehouse.com/umcor-kits/72-birthing-kits

CHAPTER 1

A Scream in the Night

"Wake up, Auntie! Wake up!"

The knocking on the door finally penetrated Rachel's sound sleep. She rolled over on her warm mat and bumped into her husband, Obadiah, who lay beside her. This jarred her aching joints, and the pain woke her up more fully. As she stood up from her pallet, her knees popped loudly in protest.

She muttered, "It's getting harder and harder." Beside her, Obadiah rolled over and protested at the noise and the draft of cold air sweeping under the blanket.

"Why do babies always come in the middle of the night?" he complained.

"Now, now," she scolded. "It might not be a new baby."

"It's always a new baby. A man can't ever get a decent night's sleep around here," he grumbled good-naturedly. He sleepily asked her, "Who is expecting this time?"

"I don't know of a single girl who is expecting and needs me to help her deliver tonight. Hannah has another three or four months, and Rebecca is even earlier than her," she replied.

1

Rachel got up, shrugged on her outer garment, and shuffled to the door. When she opened it, there was Benjamin, the young teenage son of Asa, the innkeeper. The light from his raised lantern washed over his curly black hair, sunburned face, and eyes that sparkled brightly. He looked too wide-awake and alert for this time of night.

"Aunt Rachel, my mother sent me to ask you to please come quickly. There is a young lady at the inn who needs you," he said loudly to the whole street as he bounced from foot to foot.

"Now?" Rachel asked as she tried to temporize.

"Yes, right now," he said excitedly.

"Okay, okay, I'll come," she said.

Rachel closed the door and came back inside, coiling her long, gray hair to tuck under her head covering. Her husband rose up on an elbow and muttered, "I told you so."

She shushed him and explained, "It's young Benjamin from the inn. His mother sent him, as there is a young girl in labor down there. She must have come to town with the other travelers to pay the Roman census tax."

"I wonder if her labor is due to all that riding on the donkeys to get here," Obadiah theorized.

"*Humph*, more like all that *walking* to get here," his wife muttered. "Some of these ladies have walked four days or more to get here."

"Well," he said discouragingly, "I bet they will claim that they don't have a mite to pay you after they have paid the tax."

Rachel nudged him with her bony elbow and said acidly, "That's not why I do this." She walked over to the fireplace, and kneeling down on her protesting knees, she blew into the embers until a small spark flamed into life. She used it to light a piece of straw, and from this small flame, she lit the wick of her olive-oil lantern. The weak light barely caused shadows to flicker on the walls, but her husband still moaned. She looked at him as he squinted in the light. His bushy black eyebrows were darker than his gray hair, which splayed out in every direction and contrasted sharply with his massive gray beard. He pulled the blanket over his head, as though a beam from the noonday sun had blinded his eyes. The light was just enough so that she could start gathering her supplies together. She found her bag containing her vial of olive oil, knife, precut scarlet threads, basin, and salt. Her leather apron was hanging from a wooden peg on the wall. Despite careful washing from the last use, it still rolled up very stiffly. She briefly stopped to glance at the polished bronze on the wall beside the door to see if her hair was decently covered. Although the light was poor, she could see her dark-brown eyes and accompanying crow's-feet on the outside of each eye. She wondered where the time had gone and where all the wrinkles came from.

"Now, which inn are you going to?" Obadiah asked.

"It's Asa's boy who came to tell me, so I assume they are there," she answered.

He rolled over as she slowly tied on her sandals and creaked out the door.

She saw that Benjamin was still standing by the front door and shuffling his feet anxiously. He hurried off in front of her, outdistancing her easily, but waited impatiently at each turn as though he was afraid she might lose her way. After living in Bethlehem sixty years, she could have found her way to his inn blindfolded. At this time of night, it actually was like walking blindly, as the lantern light seemed to be swallowed up by the darkness.

To slow Benjamin down, Rachel asked, "When did they arrive?"

Benjamin explained, "This evening. The pregnant lady was so exhausted she almost slid off her donkey. My father told them that the inn was full."

Rachel nodded, as she knew at this time of year, with the census, there would be no room in town for visitors unless they had relatives. She asked, "What did they do?"

"Her husband was very upset, as they had already checked several other places without any luck. He said that his wife was pregnant and needed a roof over her head during the cold night. My father was sorry but firm. He told them the inn was packed out right now, but maybe in a couple of days, they could try back," Benjamin replied.

"What changed his mind?" Rachel wondered out loud.

"My mother," replied Benjamin. "She came out, and when she saw the young lady, she felt sorry for her. She walked up beside my father and whispered to him, 'The stable.'

"My father whispered back to her, 'But the customers' animals are already in the stable.'

"My mother gave him that look," Benjamin continued. "While they were whispering, the young husband looked hopefully to my father. My father said, 'I don't suppose you'd be willing to stay in a stable.' But the young man excitedly took him up on his offer.

"Then we all walked down the hill to the small cave that serves as our stable. I slid out the poles that function as

4

the gate for the fence outside of the cave. I took out four of the donkeys and tied them to the fence poles. This gave the young lady enough room so she could lie down, although there were still several animals in the cave. Before she did, I hurriedly raked the worst of the manure out and placed some fresh straw down as a pallet. As you know, the stable stinks, but the longer you stay in there, the more your nose gets used to it. Surprisingly, the pregnant lady didn't seem to notice the smell at all, but immediately collapsed thankfully on the straw. Then my mother told me to get some water for the lady, so I ran back to the house and came back with a full gourd, which she appreciated.

"My father was anxious to leave once they were situated. As you know, he is tight with his money, so he asked my mother if he should charge them the same overnight rate as two people at the inn or a rate equal to the cost of boarding four donkeys in the stable since those donkeys had been displaced outside.

"My mother felt very sorry for the young lady and hushed him, 'They are not going to eat your straw.' Then she shooed him away. She gave them a small clay lamp, which they gratefully accepted, as it is dark in the cave, especially at night.

"The young man asked, 'Where can I buy or find a little wood to build a fire?'

"I helped him gather some dirty straw and dried dung to get the fire started outside the cave. Then we added some broken fence rails from the alley. My mother seemed reluctant to leave for some reason. I heard her say to the pregnant lady, 'Do you feel hot? Your face is red and flushed.'

"Her suspicions must have been confirmed, because when the young lady groaned and clutched her big stomach, Mother yelled at me, 'Benjamin, run and get Auntie Rachel! Now!' So I took off."

Rachel listened to Benjamin's story with interest as they picked their way through the sleeping village. She noticed that as they passed each house, the dogs woke up and questioned their passage by barking. The inn had a couple of lamps that were not extinguished yet, and this was Benjamin's focus, as they walked back and forth through the narrow streets. The cold hurt Rachel's arthritic, gnarled hands, so she grimly exercised them inside her sleeves, preparing for battle. Benjamin, with his young, energetic legs, walked too fast with his lantern, and she admonished him, "Slow down. Slow down."

Upon arriving at the hotel, Rachel followed Benjamin past it down the alley to the back of the inn and downhill to the cave. As she got closer, she could tell her services would be needed that night. She could hear moans coming from the cave, similar to what she had heard for many years working as a midwife. Her heartbeat picked up and aches faded as she came to the entrance of the cave. She could hear the moans getting louder the closer she came. The boy scurried to slide the poles aside and move the four displaced donkeys. They tugged on their ropes, stamped their feet, and rolled their eyes nervously, exposing the whites. She followed him in, instinctively ducking as she entered.

The pungent smell of donkeys, cattle, manure, urine, and straw assaulted Rachel's senses as her eyes tried to adjust to the scene in front of her. As her sandals sank into the slippery filth on the floor of the cave, she noticed that it had been widened on the inside slightly. The animals were off to the left behind some poles, and in the walkway in front of her, on a blanket-covered straw pallet, was a young girl in obvious pain. The young lady's husband stood helplessly beside her. Rachel briefly noticed that the husband was broadly built, but since his strength was useless in this situation, he huddled over his wife indecisively, uncertain of what to do.

A small clay pot with a smoldering wick gave off a feeble light. The three cows mooed nervously, and the two donkeys rolled their eyes and shuffled anxiously in the tight quarters. Because of the increased number of guests at the inn, the innkeeper had been forced to accommodate more animals than usual in the stall.

The innkeeper's wife appeared to be relieved to see Rachel and gratefully turned over her charge.

Rachel greeted her briefly. "Shalom, Tirzah." Tirzah responded in the same manner but shook her head like she doubted there would be much peace this evening.

Rachel turned and greeted the couple. "Shalom. You may call me Auntie Rachel. What is your name?" she asked as she set down her sack of supplies.

"I am Joseph bar-Jacob from Nazareth, and this is my wife, Mary," the man answered.

Rachel nodded politely to the young man. "Well, don't you worry. I have delivered many a new baby into the world, and I am here to help you tonight," she said as she smiled reassuringly at them.

Then she asked, "Mary, how long have you been hurting?"

"I started having pain in my stomach just after breakfast this morning. I thought it was something I ate. After getting on the donkey this morning, I noticed that I had wet my clothes and was surprised by this, as I didn't feel like I needed to go." She gasped in sudden pain, cutting off her story.

Rachel noticed the young man looked uncomfortable. She said, "Excuse me, sir. Could you please go with Benjamin and get us some water? David's well is in the center of town." She could tell that she would need more water than just the initial gourd. The young man didn't protest that this was a woman's job; instead, he appeared grateful and left in a hurry.

"Benjamin," Rachel called out to the teenager hovering at the entrance of the cave, "please go with this visitor and show him where the well is located." Benjamin looked reluctant to give up his watch post at the mouth of the cave to guide the man. She also called out, "Please try to bring back more wood for the fire."

She turned her attention back to the young lady and wiped her brow, waiting for the pain to pass. Once the contraction eased, Mary continued with her story, "In the morning, it seemed like the pain would hit me about once every one hundred steps of the donkey. I know this, as to take my mind off the pain, I started to count the donkey's steps between each stab of pain. But as the day progressed, it hit at seventy-five, fifty, and twenty-five steps. I don't know if the pain was coming more frequent or if it was because of Joseph."

"Joseph was causing the pain?" Rachel queried in confusion.

"No, no, but even though I tried to hide the pain, he could tell something was wrong and made the donkey move more and more quickly. He started the day holding the rope and leading the donkey by three cubits. As the day went on, he shortened his grip on the rope at two cubits and then one to pull harder on the braying donkey and cut short his protest," Mary explained.

Rachel nodded, trying to visualize Joseph walking in front approximately the distance of the height of a man and gradually drawing the rope tighter and tighter to get a better pull on the donkey.

Mary continued, "Even though I begged him to stop and rest the poor donkey, by the time we were coming up the hill to Bethlehem, he was jogging desperately beside the donkey, and then he grabbed the right side of the bridle, almost lifting the donkey's forequarters off the road. The poor donkey was sweating and too winded to protest. He was blowing white foam all over Joseph's hand as Joseph hauled him up the hill."

"Goodness!" Rachel exclaimed. "Well, don't worry now; the donkey will get his rest. It is a good thing that Joseph was so persuasive. Those waves of pain that you are feeling is your body getting ready to push the baby out. The fact that they are coming more and more frequently means your time is almost here."

Mary looked a little frightened at this and so very young.

To distract her, Rachel asked, "Mary, how old are you?"

"I have seen fourteen harvests," Mary replied. Rachel thought she looked like she was ten. The girls seemed to be getting younger and younger to her as she aged.

"How long have you been married?" Rachel asked.

Rachel noticed a slight hesitation as Mary replied, "We were engaged this summer." Rachel noticed this wasn't a direct answer to her question but decided this was not the time to delve into this discrepancy. She wondered, though, because when a woman became engaged, she was pledged to her husband. They were regarded as man and wife except that he didn't know her sexually until after their wedding. It was unusual for a woman to be pregnant during her engagement period. If she became pregnant by another man, she would be regarded as an adulteress and by law could be stoned. Occasionally, a young girl was pressured by her boyfriend or raped by a Roman soldier and became pregnant before her betrothal. Rachel remembered in the fields how the old ladies' tongues would wag and abruptly still when the object of their gossip walked up. The scorn and stigma those young ladies had to endure was crushing. She felt sorry for Mary and what she probably had to suffer through in her hometown.

"Do you have any other family with you on this trip?"

"No, just Joseph and I," whispered Mary.

Rachel tried to hide her surprise that there wasn't a mother or aunt with Mary on this trip during this critical time, but despite her attempt to guard her expression, she must have let something slip, as Mary seemed to feel it necessary to justify and defend her family's absence.

"It was only because of the Romans demanding a census at this time of year that we had to come. Joseph is a descendent of David, so he had to come here to register," she said defensively. "Joseph did not think it would be wise for me to stay by myself and my family did not realize that the baby would come so soon. They assumed we would be able to make the return journey home before the baby came."

Rachel noted that she did not include herself when she said, "They did not think the baby would come so soon."

Rachel queried gently, "Do you think it is time for the baby to come. Do you think you have been pregnant for nine months?"

The answer was not immediately forthcoming. "Don't worry, Mary," Rachel said. "Although I'm an old woman, I can keep secrets and don't go blabbing everything I'm told to the other women when we go to draw water in the morning. But I want to help you and your baby and need to know if the little one is coming on time or too early."

Mary nodded tentatively. "I think nine months have passed, but I am not sure."

That puzzling statement earned raised eyebrows of doubt from Rachel, but the next contraction caused Mary to scream for the first time.

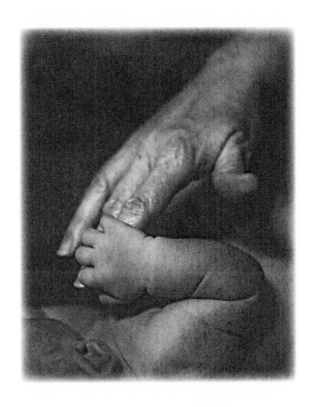

CHAPTER 2

A Natural Birth

Her yell startled the two remaining donkeys, who brayed in alarm. They stamped and kicked their hooves against the wooden partition, which set off the cows, who mooed in protest. This racket set the others heehawing outside the stable. They yanked on the ropes tied to the fence, which creaked and squeaked alarmingly. The dogs closest to the stable started barking, and not to be outdone, the others further out in the village followed suit, howling the alarm to the outskirts of the town. One or two roosters crowed loudly to prove they hadn't overslept. Rachel took small comfort that at least she would not be the only one who wouldn't be getting much sleep that night.

Mary bit down on her lip as the contraction ended and asked, "How much longer will it be?" once the wave of pain had passed.

"Oh, these things take time, but I'm here to help you," Rachel reassured Mary as she pulled the leather apron over her head. Rachel's heart went out to her for having to go through this hard experience in a strange place. She silently prayed that Mary would have the strength to keep pushing. Sometimes, young girls became exhausted, gave up, and died. Rachel soothed the girl and comforted her. Although she herself had never gone through this experience, she had helped deliver over a hundred babies through the years and knew what to expect. She didn't want to worry Mary, but she knew that sometimes, the contractions could take from half a day to three days and then the pushing could go on for three hours.

Rachel was worried about how far along Mary's labor had progressed so she continued her preparations. She pulled her skirt immodestly high to her knees so that she could kneel beside Mary. Then she tucked her sleeve above her left elbow, and skillfully using her right hand and mouth, she was able to tie it into place. Her right sleeve took longer, as her left hand wasn't as adept. This freed her arms to do the necessary exam. She checked Mary and was surprised to feel a hard, firm head at the tip of her two fingers. The baby's head was already settling in the pelvis, which was a good sign. She thought that the donkey ride must have helped Mary along in her labor, as usually, someone as young as she was and with her first baby wouldn't have progressed this quickly.

"How many children do you have?" Mary asked.

"Oh, dozens and dozens of them," Rachel replied. Seeing the confused look on Mary's face, she confided, "My husband and I weren't able to have children, but as I don't have any children or grandchildren of my own, I help every new mother with her newborn here in Bethlehem. Since you came because of the census, I assume your husband has some close relatives here?"

"No, not close. My husband's father lived in Bethlehem as a boy, but he moved to find construction work at Caesarea Philippi. My husband does construction and carpentry work now in Nazareth, but he has never actually lived here in Bethlehem. His great-uncle lives here, but he only sees him during feast days in Jerusalem."

Her talking cut off abruptly as a wave of pain washed over her.

Rachel spread her cloth on her right-hand side within easy reach and arranged her knife, strings, and salt. She saw Mary's eyes widen at the sight of the knife.

"Have you ever helped at a birthing?" she asked her.

"In the back to go and fetch things," Mary replied.

"Well, you remember when the baby comes, I will tie off the baby's cord that connects to you and then cut it, rub the child with salt, and wrap him or her tightly in cloth."

Mary nodded and asked, "Is that why you have several strings?"

"Yes, I have four—two to tie off the connecting cord on each side, one as a backup in case I break one of the first two, and the fourth to tag the child."

"But why are they red, and what do you mean by 'tag the child'?"

"This is the way it has been done for hundreds of years. Some argue that the string is red so that it is the same color as blood and therefore bloodstains won't discolor it. Others say it is traditional to use red to better label the firstborn of twins. Do you remember the story of Tamar's twins?"

Mary nodded.

"How first one twin stuck his arm out so the midwife tagged his arm with a scarlet thread, but then he withdrew it, and Perez pushed his brother Zerah aside and came out first?[2] Perez went on to become the head of the leading clan of Judah and David's ancestor. I always tie a scarlet thread around the first baby's wrist in case of the possibility of twins because you know how important it is to get the birthright to the first twin."

Mary muttered, "Well, at least I can be thankful that I don't have to worry about that."

Rachel just shook her head. "No one ever really knows. Only Rebekah was told that she would have twins." Changing the subject, she asked, "How many baby cloths were you able to bring?"

Mary pointed with her chin at a pack. She appeared to be worried about Rachel's disapproval over so few cloths, so she apologized, "We only had one donkey to carry our things, so I couldn't bring what I needed for the baby."

Rachel retrieved the cloths and laid them beside her.

Mary gasped as the pain hit her. "How much longer?"

About that time, her husband arrived carrying the basin, and Rachel placed it next to her. She dipped a cloth into it and wiped Mary's sweating face.

"I am really thirsty," Mary whispered.

Her husband filled a ladle and started to offer the water to her.

"Not too much, as we don't want her to get sick," Rachel cautioned.

Looking startled, he almost dropped the ladle.

---

[2]   Genesis 28:27–30.

"You see, the water here from King David's well is so good we don't want you to drink too much." Rachel used her words lightly so he wouldn't take her correction too much to heart.

Seeking to take her mind off the pain, Rachel asked, "Have you chosen a name for the child?"

"Yes," Mary said softly, "we know what his name will be."

Her husband squeezed her hand.

Rachel teased gently, "Oh, it's to be a boy, *eh*, and what if it's a girl? Have you picked out a name for her?"

The couple looked at each other blankly, as if this thought had never crossed their minds.

"You men," Rachel chided Joseph, "always thinking that every firstborn will be a boy and never taking any thought that the baby could just as easily be a girl."

Joseph protested, "But, you see, we were told—"

But whatever he was about to say was cut off in a gasp of pain from Mary.

Rachel thought to herself, *Yes, you were probably told by your parents or grandparents what to name the baby as a boy, but no one ever cares or makes plans on what to call little girls.*

The next wave of pain caused the girl to scream, and it reverberated loudly in the small confines of the cave. Rachel noticed the animals nervously moving as far away as possible, up next to the wall. The indignant braying and mooing hurt her ears. Even though she couldn't see much in the darkness, the whites of the animals' eyes stood out as they rolled them nervously. It was interesting to see how the donkeys' ears rotated toward Mary. Every groan of pain from her was tracked suspiciously by their ears.

Rachel had Joseph bring two flat stones and helped Mary squat on them. She took some olive oil and rubbed her abdomen and then pushed down on it when the next wave of pain came. She was glad as the labor wore on that she had delivered so many babies that she could do it with her eyes closed, as it was very dark in the cave. The anemic flame loaned to them by the innkeeper seemed to be absorbed by the darkness rather than to dispel it. Asa, the frugal innkeeper, had reluctantly let them have it, but only after threatening them with their lives if they allowed his straw and animals to be burned out.

With each wave of pain, Mary prayed, "O Lord, my strength and my shield, please protect him." As the contractions became closer together, her prayer was shortened, "O Lord ... my strength ... and my shield ... please protect him."

Finally, after what seemed like hours of pain and struggle, Rachel noticed that Mary wasn't talking or answering her questions but seemed distant. Looking into Mary's eyes, she noted that where her eyes had been slightly dilated in the gloom of the cave, now they were completely dilated. She felt like she was looking into twin black pools. She realized that Mary had progressed far along in her labor and had that faraway look in her eyes where she wasn't really seeing Rachel. She was in a place where she had lost connection with time and her whole focus was on getting the baby out.

"Push, Mary! Push!" Rachel cheered her on. "Almost there."

She examined and felt relieved when she finally felt the top of the baby's head crowning out. She relayed the good news to Mary, "Almost there. Keep pushing."

Not only was she relieved for Mary, but her arthritic hips and knees were screaming for relief as Rachel knelt in front of Mary. Rachel made certain that the cloth for the baby was still tucked into the belt that gathered her baby-delivering apron around her. When the baby's entire head broke free, Rachel supported it with her left hand. Carefully, she waited to see if the head would naturally turn to the right or left. Rachel swept her right hand around the baby's neck to ensure that there was no ill-placed cord, which might cause strangulation. She wiped the mouth with the cloth to remove any mucous that might be inhaled. Then, she gently supported the head. Slowly, the child's head rotated to the right. Although everything in her screamed to grab the head and pull the baby out by the neck to hurry and get the delivery over with after so much suspense, Rachel remembered her mentor telling her this was the most critical time to be patient. Her teacher had taught Rachel that many babies were born with limp and damaged arms because of someone pulling too enthusiastically on the neck. She prayed for strength to wait for the next contraction.

"The head is out. Come on! Push, Mary! Push!" Rachel encouraged her.

With a final groan, Mary pushed, and one shoulder, followed rapidly by the other, appeared. With a fluid motion that made light of the hard labor before, the baby came out slippery quick with a gush of water, and Rachel laid the babe in her own lap. Her cold hands must have shocked the little one, because there was a weak cry of protest. This cry was music to her ears. Instinctively, she reached for one string and waited for the pulsations in the cord to stop. Rachel remembered from her instructor's lessons that the Torah taught that the life of the body is in the blood. According to tradition then, it was vitally important that the baby received all the blood from the cord before it was tied. When all movement in the living connection ceased, Rachel quickly tied the cord in the dark and then tied the second closer to the baby's navel. She swiftly divided the cord with her knife and then dried the child quickly and transferred it to the cloth on her right.

"Excuse me, sir. Could you please bring the lamp closer?" she asked Joseph.

He laid his wife back on her pallet and held the lamp over Rachel.

Joseph asked hesitantly, "Is it all right?"

She nodded. "It's a baby boy, you have. You were right. Don't worry."

As she wiped the baby, she sensed the relief in his voice as he said, "Thank you. Thank you."

Again, she reassured him, "Look at his fine head of hair; hear his good lungs. Oh, he will make you a fine son."

A jet of urine shot up in the air as if to punctuate her remark.

"Now, now, I just wiped you," she chided the little rascal. She rubbed the baby with salt and tagged his right arm with the scarlet thread. Then she quickly wrapped the cloths around him tightly, so he would feel secure and warm.

She took a thin band of cloth and tied it around the whole bundle. Then she formally handed him to Mary and declared, "Here is your son." She gave her blessing over the child and young couple.

"Blessed are You, HaShem, our God, King of the universe, who brings forth life."

Joseph responded for both of them and pronounced the ancient blessing on the birth of a son, "Blessed are You, HaShem, our God, King of the universe, who is good and does good."

As the new mother took the baby awkwardly and gingerly, Rachel gave her some advice, "Make sure you support his head."

The little one, despite being bundled almost too tightly to move, started mewing weakly and trying to turn his head back and forth.

"Auntie, what's wrong with him?" Mary asked anxiously.

"Nothing, except he's hungry and wants to eat." Seeing her blank look, she explained, "He needs his milk."

She thought to herself, *This new mother really needs to have family here.*

She walked over, helped Mary loosen her gown, and positioned the baby where he could find his milk. Immediately, he latched on and soon was making a surprisingly loud sucking sound. The mother looked anxious, but Rachel reassured Mary, "When it seems like he isn't getting any more, then move him to the other side. After that, he will go to sleep."

"When will I know when it's time to feed him again?" she asked.

"Oh, don't you worry," she said wryly. "He will let you know."

As she said this, she noticed amusedly that the husband seemed to be somewhat embarrassed by these proceedings and had slipped outside.

Mary interrupted her thoughts. "Auntie, I don't understand, but there seems to be more pressure and bleeding," she confessed confusedly.

Rachel quickly checked her and said, "Don't worry, dear. That's just the afterbirth, and I'll take care of it." She quickly scooped it up and placed it in a pile of straw. Then she set to work cleaning her up with a wet rag.

Later, the new mother watched her newborn fondly as he finished eating and starting yawning. This started Mary yawning after her exhausting birthing battle. Cradling the baby, she asked, "Auntie, do I just put him down beside me now to sleep?"

Now, this was a problem. Occasionally, new mothers crushed their babies while sleeping. But there just wasn't any other place to put the baby in the cave. Seeing the now placid cows sticking their heads through the beams to eat their hay from the feed trough gave her an idea. She called out to Joseph, who was feeding the fire outside, "Can you help me, please? I want you to move the feed trough from over there to beside your wife."

Although the wooden trough was solidly built and heavy, Joseph moved it easily. The cows appeared to look with dismay at having their food being taken away but didn't moo in protest, as they seemed glad that all the commotion had finally stopped.

Joseph caught on to the idea and took the initiative to add more fresh straw and covered it with a blanket. The sleeping infant fit snugly. Rachel was quite pleased with herself. "I have seen the tax collector baby's crib, and this feed trough is just as comfortable as his." She chuckled.

Afterward, Rachel gathered her things together and said, "I'll come back to see you tomorrow."

She slipped outside, nodding to Mary's sleepy thanks, and threw the straw and afterbirth into the dung heap beside the alley. She washed her hands and knees with water from the basin and dried them in the cold air, thinking, *This is why I never can keep my hands from getting chapped and dry.* She took off the apron, shook out her skirt, and freed her sleeves. She noticed Joseph slipping up beside her and clearing his throat.

"Auntie, thank you so much for helping us. I don't know what we would have done if you hadn't been here."

"Don't worry; you would have done fine," she politely answered.

"Please, I don't know how much you usually get paid here in Bethlehem, but I want to show you how grateful we are for your help." Joseph fumbled for the bag at his belt.

This was the hardest part about being a midwife. She loved helping mothers deliver new lives into the world, and for the most part, this outweighed the times of sadness when a mother couldn't deliver and died in childbirth. During those times, she had to console herself with the thought that they would have died with or without her help. But it was hard to battle for two days with a young pregnant girl you had known since childhood and maybe even delivered yourself, only to lose her to exhaustion and inability to complete the delivery. If Rachel had had her way, she would have never charged for a single delivery, but Obadiah insisted that she receive compensation for all her sleepless nights and the cost of the cloths, oil, and salt she used. Also, the families valued her care and insisted she be paid. Even more difficult than accepting payment, though, was actually fixing a price.

"You don't have to pay me anything. I was glad to come and help, my son," she replied tenderly.

Respectfully but stubbornly, he insisted, "Please, I really want to."

"No, no, there really is no need," she said.

According to custom, he must ask three times and she must say something the third time, so he plowed on, "Auntie, please, at least tell me how much it cost you for your things."

She knew they were poor by the few belongings they had and that a manual laborer didn't make much, so she stated a low number that would have her husband cringing in disbelief. "My cloths and salt cost ten pennies, but what is that between you and me?"

Joseph was pleased that an understanding had been reached, and he insisted on putting double that amount in her hands.

"I will be back tomorrow, so you make sure your wife and baby stay warm. You know your wife will need to eat meat to replace her blood, so make sure you find her some chicken to eat tomorrow. You will need to contact the priest for the circumcision in eight days. Also, I'm thinking you should register for the census before your baby's name has been decided upon and he is officially born. I know the registration isn't expensive per person with just a small fee for the receipt, showing that you and your family are registered, but probably the Romans will use this for taxation, and it would be best if it showed that you only have two in your household right now."

"Thank you very much for your wise advice, Auntie." He bowed, uncommonly respectful for a man speaking to a woman.

She slowly returned home and tried to open the door quietly, but her husband heard her.

"Rachel, is that you?"

"Yes, it is," she confirmed wearily.

"Did everything go well?" Obadiah asked.

"Yes, mother and baby are doing fine."

"It took you awhile. Any problems?"

"No, just another baby being born."

As she got closer to him, he caught a whiff of her and turned around in alarm.

"You stink. Where have you been?"

"The baby was born in a stable."

27

"A stable. No wonder you stink. The manure there is at least a hand's span deep. Don't you come and sleep beside me," he muttered as he unceremoniously curled up in the blankets and slid to the other side of the pallet.

Exhausted, Rachel lay down looking forward to her warm bed and an uninterrupted sleep for the rest of the night. She sent a brief thanks heavenward to Yahweh that the baby was healthy and immediately plunged into a deep sleep.

CHAPTER 3

Excited Shepherds

From deep in her sleep, Rachel could hear the banging on the front door, but she was too tired to respond.

Beside her, Obadiah rolled over and muttered, "Someone's knocking."

When she didn't move, Obadiah finally got up and growled, "Two times in one night. No babies for two months and now, two times in one night?"

Still protesting, he shuffled to the door. "Why is it always the middle of the night?"

There was a curt "Shalom" and then the excited answering of several voices.

Obadiah came back and nudged Rachel.

She responded mechanically, "Who is in labor?"

In reply, he answered, "No one is in labor, but where did you say the baby was born tonight?"

Rachel sleepily responded, "In the stable behind Asa's inn."

"That Asa." Her husband chuckled. "Never lets an opportunity slip by without making a little extra money."

"Oh, I don't know if he is charging them," she protested, gradually waking up.

"Anyway, it's all very strange, as the shepherds from outside the village are babbling some nonsense about a messenger telling them to go see a newborn baby in a feed trough."

Rachel was puzzled. She asked, "Someone from Bethlehem told them about the newborn? But I just delivered him."

"No, I don't think so, but I can barely understand them. They are winded as if they ran all the way from the sheep pens outside of town and aren't making any sense. Because of the cold night, I think they've passed around one wineskin too many and are drunk. But it is odd for them to leave their sheep if it isn't something important. Is the baby really in a feed trough?"

"Yes," she answered, her mind whirling. "You know I've birthed babies at the well, the market, and during harvest time in the field, but this is the first time I've helped deliver a baby in the stable, and yes, we did put him in the feed trough."

"Then you had better talk with them," Obadiah said as he helped her up.

She reluctantly left her warm bed for the second time that night.

As she opened the door, her nose wrinkled up at the rank smell of sheep, and she thought, *Obadiah was right, shepherds.*

They were so excited that immediately one shepherd started asking, "Where is the baby? There is a new baby, isn't there?"

"Why do you ask?" she replied.

"We saw an angel—" one said.

He was cut off by another. "Scared the sheep to death! They almost climbed over the back wall, they were so panicked."

"Scared the sheep? Nearly scared me to death! I almost wet myself."

"We were sitting outside around the fire when the messenger in white came."

"So bright I almost couldn't see afterward."

"The messenger said, 'Today in David's city, a baby has been born.'"

Another voice cut him off, "He said that a *Savior* had been born to us and that he is Christ the Lord, and as a sign, we would find a baby wrapped in cloths, lying in a feed trough. Is there such a baby?"[3]

Suddenly, there was silence as their clamoring abruptly cut off. They all appeared to wait with an eager anticipation for the answer that would confirm their utmost longings and express a hope that they dared not utter.

Stunned, Rachel nodded her head dumbly and realizing they couldn't see her nod in the dark, said, "This evening, a baby boy was born in the stable at Asa's inn, and yes, I did wrap him up and place him in the feed trough, but the

---

[3]   Luke 2:11–12.

couple are strangers here. Tell me more. What else did he say?"

But the group heard what they needed to know and clamored to each other.

"It's true, just like he said!"

"Asa's stable, did you hear that? I know where it is. Hurry!"

As the eager group hurried off, one shepherd stayed behind briefly. "Thank you, Auntie. It was so wonderful, more messengers came and together said, 'Glory to God in the highest and on earth peace to men on whom his favor rests,' before they all disappeared." He finished with, "Sorry, I must hurry now."

Rachel shook her head as he hustled off to catch up with the noisy, clattering group. She couldn't believe that they would be so oblivious to everyone's rest as they continued to babble excitedly. They didn't seem to care at all whom they woke up. Their noisy passage down the street started all the dogs barking excitedly again.

Rachel turned, took Obadiah's heavy outer cloak off the peg by the door, and draped it over his shoulders while he stood dumbfounded beside her.

"Here, here, what are you doing?" he protested.

"You are going with them to the stable and tell me everything that happens."

"It's cold outside, and why would you believe a tale from a bunch of shepherds?" he feebly argued.

"I would be afraid not to believe," she replied as she hustled him out the door.

Belatedly, he asked, "Now what was his name again?"

"Joseph bar-Jacob," she called out to him as he left, still fumbling with his belt.

After Obadiah left, she went back to bed, but despite her exhaustion, sleep strangely did not come to her as she marveled at the words of the shepherds.

"Could it be? The Savior that has been prophesied for so many hundreds of years, the One who would come and redeem Israel, has he truly come?"

Her mind roved back over the evening and replayed the events, as she asked herself, "Was there anything out of place or unusual sounding at the delivery? Any clue to the amazing claim of the shepherds?"

All in all, she decided, it had been a rather straightforward delivery, although a strange location.

She thought Mary and Joseph seemed like a nice, hardworking young couple, and except for a common assumption the baby would be a boy, she couldn't think of anything that stood out. Did one of them say something about being told the baby would be a boy? Maybe so. She would definitely need to get to the bottom of the mystery in the morning.

★ ★ ★

Rachel woke up with a start at the closing of the door. Her husband came in fairly quietly for him and seemed more subdued and pensive.

Obadiah moved slowly into the room, threw some wood on the fire, and blew on the embers. Thoughtfully, he sat down on a wooden stool. Inwardly, Rachel groaned, recognizing he was in his storytelling mode, when what she wanted was a quick explanation to the mystery. She remembered Obadiah always said, "Every good story needs a good fire." Although she wanted to shout for him to hurry up and tell the story, knowing that pressing him would only slow him down, with outward nonchalance, she asked, "Well?"

"It was a good thing you sent me along," Obadiah said, grudgingly giving Rachel the credit for having the foresight to send him to help out. "It was easy to follow the group to the stable, as they chattered all the way there. They made a terrible racket through the village. I had to really hurry to catch up with them. As the shepherds approached the stable, they got louder and louder, and when they arrived, they sped up, charging toward the stable entrance, shouting, 'Let me see! I want to see him! I was here first!'

"The young man sitting by the fire must've thought he was being assaulted by a pack of thieves. He stood up from behind the fire in front of the cave and threw off his outer cloak. By the way, Rachel, you never told me he was so big. When he stood up, it seemed like he just kept getting bigger and bigger. He picked up his cudgel and raised it back in a defensive stance. His arms are huge; they are thicker around than my thighs. Did you notice this walking staff he carries?"

Rachel shook her head.

"His cudgel has a knot of wood on the top that is bigger than my two hands. In his hands, it could be absolutely deadly. When I picked up his staff later, I couldn't get my hand around it. It is twice as heavy as most walking sticks. When he raised that walking stick up, I thought somebody was about to die. He looked as lethal as a Roman legionnaire who puts his right hand on his sword hilt when he is fed up with talking. The young husband definitely looked as though he could break more than a few heads in the defense of his family. Since I thought you had already done enough work tonight and didn't want to be binding up any heads, I yelled, 'Shalom! Shalom!'

"It was difficult for me to push my way to the front of the group as the thick-headed shepherds in the front finally began to realize the danger they were in and recoiled. However, the ones behind couldn't see and were pushing the front row right toward the upraised club.

"'Joseph bar-Jacob!' I shouted. 'I am the husband of Aunt Rachel, and my eager neighbors here have forgotten their manners in welcoming guests to our village.' At this, the group stopped pushing and had the decency to look shamefaced.

"I continued, 'I am sorry to disturb your rest. Aunt Rachel didn't tell these men that your wife just had a baby tonight. Instead, they are shepherds who were asleep at their pens in the fields. They have an urgent message, which they would like to share with you if they may please.' I turned to the group and raised one finger to indicate only one spokesman.

"The oldest in the group pushed himself forward and introduced himself. 'Friend, I'm sorry we came upon you so unexpectedly. We have been blessed with some amazing news tonight. May we share why we couldn't wait to see you tonight? I think you will understand.'

"Joseph nodded and put down his staff, and the tension dropped noticeably.

"'This evening, we guarded the sheepfolds outside of Bethlehem. As you know, we take our job seriously, since many of our sheep are chosen for the Temple sacrifices in Jerusalem. While our sheep slept quietly in their pens, we watched the gates. Suddenly, a man appeared in the sky. His appearance terrified us, and then he spoke, "Do not be afraid!"

"'But we were frightened to death. It isn't every night someone suddenly appears in the sky with a bright shining light around him. We would have run away if we could; we were that scared, but there was such a sense of awe about the angel that we fell facedown.'"

Obadiah related that at this point, Joseph interrupted gently and said, "'Didn't try to frighten you, but you couldn't help it because of who he was, right?'"

"The spokesman nodded eagerly in affirmation, 'Yes, that's exactly right. The angel told us, "This evening, in the city of David, a baby has been born who will be the Savior of the world; as a sign you will find him wrapped in cloths and lying in a manger."

"'Then, beside him, all around him in the sky, there were dozens, hundreds, maybe even thousands of bright men shouting, "Glory to God in the highest and on the earth peace, goodwill to men."[4]

"'Then, just as suddenly as they appeared, they were gone. Well, after that, we stayed facedown a little longer just in case the angels returned. When it was finally clear that they were really gone, we slowly stood up. We hurried to the sheep and tried to calm them, as they had all piled up at the back wall of the pens bleating unhappily. Once the sheep settled down and after some of us had gone to relieve ourselves, we gathered back around the fire. We discussed what had just happened. All of us felt that we should investigate what we had been told. Everyone wanted to come and search for the baby who had just been born, but lots were drawn so one was selected to remain behind on guard duty. Then we hurried into town and decided to ask the midwife, Aunt Rachel, if she knew of any new baby boys born tonight. She told us of your son.

"'Is it true that you placed him in the feed trough?' At this, Joseph nodded slowly."

Obadiah looked at Rachel and commented, "You know, he didn't seem quite as perturbed as I would have been if I had just been told my son is to be the Savior of the world. He must have a very easygoing personality, because I would have been much more excited to receive such news."

Then Obadiah continued his narration.

---

[4] Luke 2:14.

"After considering this request, Joseph stepped inside the stable and there was a hurried conference. His wife must also have agreed because he came back out and nodded their permission.

"Joseph stipulated, 'The baby is sleeping, but you can come in quietly, only two at a time. Please do not wake him up.'

"The first two oldest shepherds crowded into the stable. There, they saw the tiny baby sleeping in the manger by the weak lamplight. Joseph stood by the side of the manger carefully holding his stick, in case any of these lunatics forgot themselves. But in contrast to their earlier excitement, they stood quietly and reverently as they stared down at the baby with solemn respect. Spontaneously, they both dropped to their knees and touched their foreheads to the straw of that filthy floor, giving deep homage as though they were in a palace before the emperor. When the spokesman finally stood, he turned and faced Joseph. He placed his hand on his hip where the angel had touched Jacob's hip and solemnly swore, 'My house is your house.' The second man stood up and did the same thing—touched his hip and promised, 'My family is your family.' After they stepped out, this scene was repeated for all the shepherds." Obadiah had been intrigued to hear what the teenage shepherd would say, as he had no home or family yet. "He stood up with glistening eyes and swore, 'My life for his.' They left quietly and seemed satisfied. After they left, I nodded to the couple and took my leave.

"It is rare that I envy shepherds sitting out on cold hillsides. You know, they are smelly, dirty, and people accuse them of chasing their sheep until they become like their animals—completely without manners or civilized behavior, babbling, and running in every direction. But tonight, I wanted to be one of them. I wished I had seen what they had seen and had their faith. I wish I could believe like them," he said wistfully.

Rachel could hear the regret and longing in his voice. She hugged him. "The sky is lightening, and the roosters are beginning to crow. It's too late to go back to bed. Let me fix you some bread, and I will take a loaf to the young couple this morning."

CHAPTER 4

Unexpected Visitors

It was fall, a time of feasting and celebration. The olives were ripe, and everyone turned out to pick them at the grove. Sheets were spread under the trees as children scampered up the branches and jumped with enthusiasm, showering the protesting adults below. From the fields, a steady stream of regal ladies walked back to the olive press with olive baskets perched confidently on their heads. Laughter and excitement filled the air as the first baskets were stacked under the stone-weighted beam. The strongest men used their legs to push down on the beam and then released their end simultaneously. The other end fell and struck the baskets with a satisfying squish, releasing transparent, yellow liquid that trickled and ran down through the weave of the basket into the catchment trough. Cheers went up at this, and the men were encouraged to push down harder. Suddenly, there was a crack and a groan as the beam shuddered but didn't move. This beam, as thick as a man's thigh, had broken after the past year's disuse and its drying out in the sun. Shouts of "Joseph! Joseph!" filled the air.

In the grove, Joseph was laughing with Mary as they watched little Yeshua, toddling around with his hands up, futilely trying to catch the rain of olives. He earnestly leaned over, successfully captured one, and popped it in his mouth. Mary instantly scurried over to him. "No, no, no," she corrected, as she picked him up and fished it out of his mouth.

"Joseph," she asked gently, "what are we going to do about Benjamin's gift?"

"I don't know. Put it out of his reach?" he suggested hopefully.

"It isn't that I'm worried that Yeshua will get tangled up in the cords or choked by the sling, but it's Benjamin's expectation that he will teach Yeshua to use it as well as David, the shepherd boy, did against the Philistines. What if Yeshua feels he needs to use it against the Romans? I also don't like the swordplay with sticks. Whenever I see Benjamin whacking away at him, I am worried that Yeshua will take his stick after a Roman soldier passing through town."

Joseph nodded solemnly in agreement. Whatever he was going to say was cut off by the arrival of a panting teenager explaining the predicament at the press. Joseph strode away quickly to inspect the damage.

After looking at the cracked beam, Joseph returned to his workshop where he had a similar log. Joseph told the teenager to bring his ax from the workshop. Grunting slightly, he hunched down and picked the beam up. Joseph's muscles strained and rippled as he carefully carried the replacement beam back. He didn't have time to drive a wooden peg through the center of the beam but carefully notched it and tied it to the fulcrum. This jury-rigged repair held up as the stone weights were added, and soon, the beam was squeezing life-giving oil again.

Rachel, standing in the shade of an olive tree, watched his repair work with a self-satisfied smile and turned to Obadiah.

"Isn't it great that Joseph could repair the beam?" she asked smugly.

"I suppose you are still claiming credit for inviting Joseph and Mary to stay in town," he answered.

Rachel grinned wickedly at her husband but decided to keep her thoughts to herself. A year and a half earlier, when she'd managed to convince her brother-in-law that he needed a new tenant, it had felt wonderful to help the young couple. The way Rachel saw it, the benefits had worked both ways. Joseph was an excellent carpenter, and having him move to Bethlehem had turned into a blessing for Rachel's village.

As if he'd read her mind, Obadiah continued, "My nephew was not thrilled to have to find another place to live, and it took quite a bit of convincing for my brother to accept your creative rent for the house."

"Oh, the half shekels and half repair work on the shutters and doors. Well, I knew Joseph couldn't afford the yearly rent, but the improvements he made on the house easily compensate your brother."

Obadiah raised a bushy eyebrow and said, "Not to hear him complain. You would think I had cheated him blind by suggesting this unusual arrangement. Anyway, my brother said they didn't want to go back to Nazareth, because of all the comments there about Mary being pregnant before her marriage."

With flashing eyes, Rachel tore to Mary's defense. "There isn't a sweeter or kinder girl than Mary—"

"Hold, hold, hold! I agree with you. I think it worked out well for everyone that they decided to live here," he said soothingly. "I am glad Joseph returned back to Nazareth to retrieve his tools and set up business here."

"Yes, where Yeshua can grow up in the City of David," she said significantly.

Although they did not often discuss the circumstances surrounding the night of Yeshua's birth, Rachel knew that, like she did, Obadiah frequently thought back to the shepherds' visit and declaration.

"I was surprised to hear them select that name at the time of circumcision, especially since no one in their family had the same name," he admitted. "In this volatile political situation, I can think of nothing good that will come of it."

"Why?" asked Rachel. "What's wrong with a name that means 'Yahweh is salvation'? I like it."

"There are many zealots running around claiming to be a 'savior' and calling for the death and the overthrow of the Romans. I worried about the tales the shepherds were spreading at the ceremony that someone might use them to promote rebellion. For so many shepherds to come to a strange child's circumcision really caused tongues to wag, and I am glad that things have finally calmed down," Obadiah concluded.

Fuming, Rachel turned on him. "It wasn't just the shepherds. What about the words that good man Simeon spoke just before he died, when he saw the baby for the first time at the purification rite at the Temple: 'My eyes have seen your salvation, which you have prepared in the sight of all people, a light for revelation to the Gentiles and for glory to your people Israel.'"

"If I had one denarius for every time someone claimed the Messiah had arrived to defeat the Romans, I would be a wealthy man," Obadiah said dismissively.

"What about Anna? Didn't she give the same prophecy at that time?"

"Senility comes to all of us."

"Senility comes to some earlier than others, you crazy old goat," Rachel huffed under her breath.

"Hear, hear now," he protested. "My hearing hasn't failed me yet."

As Rachel turned in frustration to go to prepare supper, she noticed a stir in the crowd. The people were moving and looking toward the road to Jerusalem in the north. The setting sun from the west highlighted a caravan approaching Bethlehem. This was unusually late in the day for visitors to be traveling, and it was rare for a caravan this large to come to Bethlehem. It wasn't a festival day, so it couldn't be pilgrims, and Bethlehem certainly wasn't on the King's Highway. The sun reflected off flashing armor and glittering harnesses as the horses approached. People started pointing out what they could see and chattered in earnest. Strangers could mean danger. Several men looked pointedly at the tax collector to see if he was responsible for calling a Roman raid on the town for back taxes. He held up his hands, indicating he was just as perplexed as they were.

Rachel thought the group seemed too well organized and prosperous to be a band of thieves. However, she was nervous, as were the women around her. They all made sure their heads were well-covered and rounded up their children. Being older, Rachel stayed behind, but she approved of the younger women who knew it was better to be at home and shepherded their children to safety so they didn't get trampled under hoof. Rachel was surprised when the caravan stopped just outside the village gates.

The village head elder, standing at the gate, appeared unsure if they were camping there or needed shelter for the night, so he sent a runner to inquire about their purpose. Rachel noticed that Asa sent his son Benjamin, over his protests, to hurry back to the inn, to warn his wife of possible guests and to place fresh straw in the stable.

Rachel was curious to hear what the messenger would say. Obadiah had joined the other village elders, as he was one of the representatives who met at the gate. Rachel moved as close as she could to the group. The runner returned and explained that the interpreter accompanying this group of foreigners said that they came in peace from a land to the east. They had just stayed in Jerusalem five miles away and now planned to spend the night here at Bethlehem.

"Where are they going?" someone piped up. "This is not the King's Highway."

The runner replied with a little frustration, "I asked the interpreter that, but something must have been lost in translation, as they just kept repeating they had come to Bethlehem and they were going to spend the night here."

"Are they coming into the village, or will they stay outside?" asked Asa, who seemed concerned about missing possible business.

"They said they were coming, but they had to prepare first."

"Prepare for what?" asked a curious observer.

"I don't know," said the messenger, "but they were taking their packs down, changing their worn and dusty cloaks for finer clothes, and pouring oil on their hair and beards."

"Foreigners have strange customs," someone observed. "They act like they are just arriving at Jerusalem instead of leaving it."

★ ★ ★

People started drifting away from the village gate as the crackling of twigs signaled the beginning of the supper fires being coaxed back to life. Obadiah followed Rachel home through the gray fog of smoke gathering over the village. He heard the doves in the trees coo to one another to confirm it was time to settle on their perch for the night. He noticed the teenagers stayed at the gate until the last possible moment, hoping to catch a glimpse of the exotic strangers. Most people hurried home; the smell of hot olive oil on iron plates and pungent smoke started floating through the village, reminding them of hungry stomachs.

Obadiah had just finished the good meal Rachel had prepared when he heard the call of an unusually shrill horn. He hurried to join the elders of the village at the gate. They all assumed correctly that this signaled the strangers' approach and were rewarded by the sight of a procession slowly walking to the entrance.

At the gate, Obadiah and the village elders stood in a group to welcome them.

The chief elder called out to the procession, "Hail, strangers! Our humble village offers you hospitality. Peace to you."

The interpreter standing beside the three magnificently robed men at the front of the column whispered quickly to them. The oldest man with a beautiful oiled gray beard bowed and solemnly called out his greeting, "Peace to you and your households." The interpreter translated quickly. He added, "The learned scholars of …" and rattled off their names and countries of origin. Seeing the blank looks of his audience, he amended this to, "… lands far to the east, have traveled for almost two long years to come to give honor and respect to Him, who has been born King of the Jews."

This astounding announcement caused confusion among the men of the village. Obadiah turned to his friend and asked, "Have you heard if Herod just had a son?"

His friend gave a negative shake.

Before Obadiah could ask another question, the oldest scholar continued to speak and pointed at the sky over the village behind them. Several people turned their heads but didn't see anything except the evening stars starting to shine out.

The interpreter continued, "According to our ancient writings, which we have studied, the appearance of a bright, new, celestial body means the birth of a new king. When we first saw this new star appear almost two years ago, by its location and other writings, we deduced that a new king has been born here in the land of the Jews."

This really caused a stir. Obadiah's neighbor asked him, "Are they saying that a prince was born two years ago?" Obadiah shrugged helplessly.

The interpreter translated again, "After seeing the star, we realized this was a very momentous occasion and decided we had to come and worship him."

Obadiah's neighbor asked him again, "Are they talking about Herod? Is that why they went to Jerusalem—to worship Herod? Who else would be called King of the Jews?"

"If they came all this way to worship Herod, I don't think much about their wisdom writings," Obadiah replied.

His neighbor speculated, "Do you think they read the ancient writings of the prophet Samuel and haven't realized that King David of Bethlehem is dead?"

Another neighbor beside them perked up his ears as he specialized in selling slings, round rocks, old lyres, and broken, rusty blades to gullible pilgrims seeking heirloom treasures of David's days in Bethlehem. He sensed the possibility of significant sales to these strangers.

Obadiah saw Benjamin jumping up and down in excitement. "Yes, this is just like the time the Queen of Sheba came with gold and gifts to honor King Solomon." He also noticed one of the shepherds from the fields leaning on his staff and seeming to nod thoughtfully.

The interpreter's translation of the stranger's speech was stilted and painful to follow, but the following words sent a cold chill through the crowd. "In Jerusalem, we were granted an audience with your respected ruler, the honorable King Herod. He was very gracious, and although he said no new ruler had recently been born in the capital city, he called your high priest and other learned scribes, who read from your ancient writings these words,

> But you, Bethlehem, in the land of Judah,
> Are by no means least among the rulers of Judah;
> For out of you will come a ruler
> Who will be the shepherd of my people Israel ...[5]

"He told us to come here and make a careful search for the child so that when we find him, we can report back to him and he can also come and worship him."

A visible shudder went through the crowd as everyone knew how paranoid Herod was, even killing his own wife, sons, and family if he had the slightest suspicion of them trying to supplant him. Even the Roman emperor had reportedly said, "I would rather be Herod's pig than his wife," insinuating you would have a better chance of living if you weren't part of his family.

"This is not good," thought Obadiah. Then, he realized he must have spoken out loud, as his neighbor nodded. "If Herod thinks there is a new ruler in Bethlehem, there will be many spies coming to try to locate him. Life will be hard

---

[5]   Micah 5:2.

as a futile search will last many days with strangers coming in to stir up unnecessary trouble."

While he was thinking this, he noticed the leader pointing to the horizon again and motioning a servant forward. Obadiah looked down the street to the west where the twilight was deepening into dusk. Only the evening star could be seen coming out as well as the new star. He remembered one of the shepherds pointing out the star several months ago and asking a Levite in town what it meant. The shepherd was worried that it might be foretelling an adverse event like an earthquake or drought or possibly a political event like a Maccabean uprising against Herod or the Zionists attacking the Romans. The Levite had reassured him that many new stars came and went without any meaning, and up to then, it appeared to be true. The star had slowly moved across the night sky toward the west each night, and it appeared on track to disappear over the horizon soon. Now it could barely be seen over the rooftops on the west side of town.

The servant brought forward a wooden box with great care. He opened it reverently, and the leader took out an unusual, shiny metal instrument with two arms. Obadiah had never seen anything quite like it. It looked like an instrument Joseph might use to measure a door or wall to see if it was straight, like a plumb line but much more ornate. It was unfolded so one arm pointed to the horizon and the other pointed perpendicularly straight up. Slowly, with the help of his two friends, the man aimed the perpendicular arm lower and lower until it was almost horizontal. He sighted down the arm like he was aiming an arrow at the horizon, right down the street.

Obadiah looked down the street due west and noticed how warm and welcoming the town looked that night. It was more brightly lit with lanterns glowing from every window and opened door. He guessed it was due to celebrating the harvest of olive oil. They could all be so extravagant with their lanterns. The street was as brightly lit as during the feast of Purim. He could see at the end of the street where the road forked north and south and the bright light coming from his brother's house spilled out on the street. He noticed that Joseph, after initially checking out the guests, had returned home at supper to work in the cool of the evening. He appeared to be putting a fulcrum through the center of the olive press beam. *He is a hard worker,* Obadiah thought approvingly. He glanced up and idly noted the new star glowing brightly in the fading light about two cubits above Joseph's house at the end of the street from where he was standing.

A chill went through him when he realized over whose house the star was located, and he hoped no one else had noticed what he had seen for the first time. There hadn't been a prince in Bethlehem since the time of David, but what if ...

His worst fears and yet best hope were confirmed when he saw the other two scholars line up behind the instrument and look directly down the street. They nodded in affirmation to the leader's question, congratulated each other after consulting a scroll, and put the instrument back in its box. With broad smiles, a shouted command was given and three strong servants came forward with a package to accompany each one of the scholars as they slowly started a solemn march down the center of the street, followed by the rest of their entourage. Although the village elders seemed uncertain of what to do, Obadiah thought he knew where they were going and started walking in front of the group. The elders eventually followed and caught up to the three leaders, trying to ask questions in a low tone to the interpreter.

Apparently, Obadiah was not the only one who sensed the strangers' ultimate destination. Benjamin, uninhibited by his youth, like a stone flung straight from a sling, broke into a dead run. As he tore by the doorways, he startled the dogs, who started their protective barking, drawing the ladies and children to the open windows to gape at the parade. Obadiah found himself involuntarily moving down the street to his brother's house and wondering what was about to happen. Seeing the shepherd outpace him with the swift strides of his long legs headed toward Joseph's house, he was reminded of the first night he had met Joseph and remembered the shepherds' reaction to the baby. Surely, it wasn't happening again.

He could see Benjamin excitedly giving a quick explanation to Joseph through the open workshop door and then urgently pulling him to the door, even though Joseph was bigger. When Joseph came to the door and saw the amazing procession approaching him, he quickly stepped over to the door of their house. Mary pulled him in, adjusted his robe from where he had tucked it up to work, and brushed some wood shavings off his arm. Obadiah arrived at the house before the head of the procession by walking much faster than he was used to. Breathing heavily, he noticed darkly that the shepherd had already staked his claim on the one window to the house so he could have a good look at whatever was about to happen. Obadiah stopped at the open door, and caught by the approaching crowd, he was uncertain of what he should do. Looking in, he saw Rachel was already there cleaning the house.

He called out, "Rachel!" and pretending that he had been diligently looking for her, came on in. She smiled at him sweetly, seeing through his fake excuse to come in and stand beside her at the back. He was a little surprised that the room looked so clean. Although Mary was a good housekeeper, little Yeshua generally kept the place cluttered, strewn with all the toys Joseph had carved for him. The bed mat was rolled up to give more room. It seemed as though Mary had prepared for company, but he didn't know how she would have known that guests were coming, as it was obvious that Joseph was just as surprised as he was. Why did he always feel a little slow when others, like Rachel, seemed to know exactly what was going on?

By the dogs barking, he knew that the procession had arrived outside. Two of the elders called a greeting and asked if they could come in. Mary stood up and looked down as they entered. They gave a brief explanation and asked Joseph's permission for the guests to enter. Confused, Joseph glanced at Mary, who nodded.

The eldest entered, and although one might have expected someone of his obvious high social status to turn up his nose at the simple house, he came in and bowed respectfully to Joseph and Mary. He said with good intention but badly accented Aramaic, "Shalom." He looked with keen interest at Yeshua and smiled at the child who was peeking out shyly from behind Mary's dress. Obadiah wondered if this toddler met the expectations of these men from the east after such a long and dangerous journey. He was followed by the other two foreigners and the interpreter. Obadiah randomly thought, *Well, at least this is brighter than the stable,* as Mary had three clay lamps burning, and it looked like Rachel had brought their lantern.

The three scholars introduced themselves, and the interpreter said, "Hail, we have come to see He who has been born King of the Jews!"

There was a shocked silence.

Poor Joseph, Obadiah thought. *He looks as confused as I feel.*

Mary, however, had a calm serenity as she absorbed this incredible statement from the men.

When they said, "King of the Jews," it seemed ludicrous that this child, who had finally been coaxed out from behind Mary's skirts, could be their king. Yeshua was fascinated by the men's unusual and brightly colored robes, and they in turn expressed their honor and joy in finally getting to meet him. With smiles, they bowed down low and worshipped before the child. Obadiah had never felt the need to bow before Yeshua, but seeing their deep reverence, he felt humbled and his knees weakened.

Then the oldest stranger called for his servant, who entered an already crowded room. He was strong but struggling with a small, heavy chest. The eldest presented the chest forward to Joseph, waving his arm toward the child. As in a dream, Joseph numbly opened the chest, and instantly, the room became brighter as the gold inside reflected the lamplight brightly. Joseph glanced wildly at Mary for reassurance. The interpreter translated, "This is a small gift for the King. Long may he live." The toddler was attracted to the color and walked over to the box, picked up a coin, and ran it back to Mary. When he tried to taste it, the scholar laughed uproariously and nodded approvingly as Mary took it out of his mouth.

The second scholar called, and another servant came with a beautiful alabaster jar. He explained, and the interpreter translated, "From my homeland to your King." He nodded to the servant who struggled to open the plug that had been set two years before. When he finally opened it, the fragrance of frankincense filled the room. Yeshua wasn't as impressed with this gift and wrinkled his nose in annoyance as the unusual scent spread. Through the window, Obadiah could hear the shouted word, "Frankincense!" as the shepherd at the window relayed outside what he could see unfolding inside.

The third man gave a beautiful jar filled with myrrh, which also gave its fragrant aroma to the house. Not only was the perfume overpowering, but it was extremely costly.

The village elder met Obadiah's eye, and he could tell what he was thinking. Joseph just went from being a middle-class laborer, to one of the richest men in town. Obadiah could see that Joseph, however, hadn't made this connection but was still trying to wrap his mind around the fact that these men had journeyed hundreds of miles to honor his son. Each of the visitors, after asking Joseph's permission, placed a hand on Yeshua's head and said a blessing in his own tongue.

They thanked Joseph and Mary and bowing low, left with beaming smiles after accomplishing their difficult mission.

Joseph and the village elders walked the men to the village gate and after thanking them, sent them away in peace. The scholars encamped just outside of town. Obadiah noticed the shepherd walking away with the interpreter and wondered if he was going to relate his previous personal experience about what he had seen the night of the baby's birth.

As the village elders started to disperse, Rachel came up to Obadiah and said, "Tell them before they separate."

"Tell them what?" he asked.

"Herod is going to hear of this, since he asked them to return. Tell the men of the town that to protect everyone here, the story of these visitors' arrival needs to be that they camped and left without anything happening."

Again, Obadiah marveled at her wisdom and called out to the men, "Excuse me, fellow elders." When they came back together, he diplomatically shared with them Rachel's concerns. "These are politically troubled times; I think it would be best if we all agree that this visit never took place tonight. These foreigners came, camped outside the gate, and then left. We don't know why they came or where they went."

Obadiah looked around and saw all their heads nodding in agreement as they discussed the proposal. Finally, they agreed this was a good idea and went home for the night. It had been a long evening.

CHAPTER 5

An Unthinkable Choice

At first light the next morning, before breakfast, Rachel picked up her clay water pot and hurried to David's well. She couldn't wait to meet Mary to discuss the night's events. This was the best time of the day for the ladies to get together and exchange news. Usually, the early arrivals stayed and helped the others to lower and raise the heavy vessels, while catching up on all the latest gossip. She wasn't surprised to find almost every lady in the village already at the well this morning after the events of the previous night.

When she walked up, two or three ladies immediately came over to help her.

"Rachel, shalom!" they called out.

"Shalom," she replied, knowing that what they were really saying was, "What did you see last night?"

About that time, a man came by hurrying to the house of the chief village elder. Knocking on the door, he blurted out, "They're leaving." The village elder came out quickly tying his outer robe. They hurried off, and the women immediately left their water vessels by the well and followed them. The ladies stopped at the gate while the men continued down to the campsite as the caravan was forming up. Rachel saw Obadiah and the other village elders hurry down in ones and twos. Soon, the caravan lined up and headed south as the elders waved their farewell.

When the elders returned, they were confronted by their wives. Rachel found Obadiah and asked him, "Why are they leaving by the southern road?"

Obadiah replied, "We asked them the same question, wondering if they were lost, as that was the wrong road to go back to Jerusalem. The interpreter explained that during the night, one of the scholars had a vivid dream. In the dream, he was warned that they should not go back to Herod to report what they had found. Instead, they should go home another way.[6] This made them very happy and confirmed to them the success of their mission."

Rachel said delightedly, "Isn't this wonderful? Now we don't have to worry about them reporting back to Herod."

Obadiah agreed, "This is good news, but we must still be careful."

★ ★ ★

That evening, it seemed like they had just dropped off to sleep when there was an urgent pounding on the door. "Hello? Obadiah. This is Joseph. Open up."

Obadiah rolled over in bed. "Rachel, they're calling you; someone must be in labor. Why can't I get any sleep?" he complained loudly.

---

[6] Matthew 2:12.

Feeling immediately alarmed, Rachel groped for her wrap and called out, "I'm coming."

Is Mary or Yeshua sick? she wondered as she hurried to the door. It was odd, she thought, for Joseph to come and get her at this hour. She opened the door and saw him standing out there.

"May I please speak to Obadiah?" he asked quickly.

She invited him in and mentally apologized for feeling gleeful that it was Obadiah who was being called out. She nudged him. "You are wanted."

"What?" Obadiah asked in bewilderment.

He shuffled to the door where Joseph was waiting.

"What is the trouble?" he asked.

"Mary and I must leave tonight."

"What?"

"I have been told to take my family away. Herod is going to search for Yeshua to try to kill him," Joseph explained.[7]

"Who told you? Do you have a friend in the palace?" Obadiah asked.

Joseph looked Obadiah directly in the eyes. "An angel told me in a dream tonight to leave immediately."

Shocked, Obadiah looked around. He had always thought of Joseph as a steady, levelheaded kind of fellow, not given to flights of fancy, and now this amazing statement.

Joseph explained, "This is the second time an angel has spoken to me. When an angel told me to take Mary as my wife, I did so immediately. I need to obey right away."

Obadiah was stunned. For the past four hundred years, the prophets had been silent. No angels had appeared during

---

[7] Matthew 2:13.

that time, and this young carpenter now claimed that an angel had spoken to him—twice!

Obadiah retreated back to what he knew. "Well, you're right to leave. I was afraid it might come to this, as Herod is so paranoid. After the parade the day before yesterday, he will be very anxious to remove any threat to his throne."

Obadiah wasn't too surprised to hear Rachel speak up from behind his back where she had heard every word. "We will come over immediately to help you pack."

Joseph nodded and left.

Obadiah turned to Rachel. "We will?"

"Poor Mary! She and Joseph must be so worried! Will Yeshua be safe?" Rachel wondered worriedly.

Her shoulders stooped. She covered her face with her hands. Obadiah put his arm around her to reassure her, saying, "God will protect them. Look at the dream He sent."

"But how are they going to pack all their belongings on their one donkey? They'll need at least two," she thought out loud.

"You're right," said Obadiah. "What do you want me to do?"

"Wait. Let me think." Rachel pulled on her robe and slipped on her sandals. "Obadiah, go over to Asa's and tell him to bring one of his donkeys. Oh, and some silver."

Obadiah asked, "Should I try and get three or four donkeys? Joseph can afford them now."

"No," Rachel explained. "Even if they could each handle two donkeys, it would look strange for one couple to be handling a caravan of donkeys. They don't need to attract any attention."

Rachel hurried over to Mary and Joseph's house after putting some supplies in a bag and embraced a teary-eyed Mary. Little Yeshua was sleeping on his mat through the flurry of preparations. She explained to them, "In this bag are flat bread, dried meat, and three dried cakes of figs. I have also included one wineskin. I wish I had more."

"Thank you, Auntie. This is too much; we can't accept it," Mary protested.

"Nonsense, it's what neighbors are for," Rachel replied. "Are you taking two outfits of clothes for yourselves and several for the child?"

"Yes, ma'am."

"Good."

"We will miss you so much," Mary said.

Rachel felt her eyes start to tear, but about that time, Obadiah, Benjamin, and Asa arrived. Asa was complaining almost as much as the donkey, who didn't want to leave his warm stall.

Rachel said, "Asa, Joseph and Mary want to buy your donkey."

Asa protested, "But this donkey is like one of my own family; I can't bear to part with a family member."

"But if the price was right ..." Obadiah muttered, until a sharp elbow from Rachel shut him up.

Eventually, the transaction was completed. "Now, Asa, change one of Joseph's gold coins into silver so he doesn't have to show any of the gold on his trip," Rachel commanded.

"Without scales and I don't even recognize the image?" Asa looked scandalized.

But even this difficulty was overcome. "Make sure you put the jars of perfume in bags of meal to cushion and to hide them. Try to keep most of the coin on both your persons, and don't put both jars on the same donkey, in case he runs away. Do you have one small pot for cooking? Keep your fire tender dry …" Rachel continued to shower them with suggestions. She insisted on hugging and kissing the sleeping Yeshua before saying good-bye.

Joseph and Obadiah walked out to the workshop one last time. Joseph reluctantly ran his hands over his tools—the adze, planer, hammer, and wedge—wishing desperately he could take them but knowing their size and weight made it impossible. He picked up an ax for firewood.

"You can afford to buy other tools," Obadiah offered.

Joseph nodded. "But some of these were my father's and he taught me how to use them."

"I will store them," offered Obadiah.

"Thank you," answered Joseph. "These smaller ones …" He gestured to those on his workbench. "Please send by caravan to Nazareth, as I have some relatives there who can use them." Obadiah nodded his assent.

"Now it is probably best that we don't know where you are going so we can truly deny it, but if you go to the Jewish enclave in Alexandria, I know a couple of men there. With the money you have, you can settle in almost any part of the Roman Empire. Try to find a place with a Jewish community. It is important you go outside the influence of Herod. I realize that David's parents fled to Moab when he was in hiding, but you should go further than that," Obadiah counseled.

Joseph nodded as they walked back to the two waiting donkeys. After an emotional good-bye among the ladies, the couple walked off into the night with Yeshua strapped to Mary's back.

The room, which held so many warm memories, seemed forlorn and bare. Rachel looked around and clapped her hands. "Now to work."

"What?" Asa and Obadiah stared at her dumbfounded. "We have been working. What are you talking about?"

"We need to trash this house so that it looks deserted and broken down," she replied.

"Why?"

"When those scholars don't return to Herod," she answered, "he will be upset and angry. He will probably send his spies to scout out the village. This house must look like no one has lived in here for months."

Asa put minimal effort into the new renovation because of his laziness. Obadiah didn't get much accomplished because he kept wondering what his brother would say when he found out they had destroyed his house. However, Benjamin jumped into it with a will and made up for their lack of effort with youthful enthusiasm. He tore down the shutters Joseph had added, pulled the door out of its joint, and brought in straw and manure. He also brought in a couple of cows to stake out in the house and two donkeys for the workshop. Rachel nodded in satisfaction.

"In a couple of days, it will smell like no one has lived in here for years."

They trudged tiredly to their beds and fell into a dead sleep just as the rooster began to crow.

★ ★ ★

Two nights later, Herod struck. The soldiers came bursting into the room. "Where's the midwife?" they yelled gruffly. Seeing only the elderly couple, they grabbed each one of them. They shook Rachel roughly, knocking her cowl off and freeing her graying hair to fly in every direction.

"Who in this village has baby boys? Tell us where all the baby boys are. If you don't, we will kill the old man."

One of the soldiers stuck his sword against the side of Obadiah's neck and made a small nick. Rachel muffled a scream as she saw the blood trickling down through his beard. Were they going to kill Obadiah? Those soldiers were serious! She couldn't bear it if they hurt her beloved husband! Desperately she began to pray, but then her mind went blank and all she could do was repeat, "Babies? Babies?"

Obadiah looked at her steadily and said, "I believe. I believe ..."

Instantly, with the clarity of forty years of marriage, she could tell that he was telling her he would gladly give his life to keep the baby's secret safe.

Her mind raced in every direction as she tried to think of a solution out of their situation, but all the while, she could only say, "Babies? Babies?" Praying fervently to the God of Israel, she asked, "Give me the wisdom you gave Shiphrah and Puah when Pharaoh demanded they explain why they were not killing the newly born Israelite boys. Those midwives were wise and gave him an answer he believed.[8] O Lord, what did our David do when King Saul tried to kill him? When David was called before the Philistine king, what did he do?"[9] Then it hit her.

She already looked a sight, her gray hair frizzed in every direction, eyes rolling desperately and idiotically while she repeated, "Babies, babies ..." She turned to look at Obadiah, crossed her eyes, and let her jaw go slack, praying he would get the message.

The soldier seemed frustrated by her lack of intelligible response and shook Obadiah roughly. His eyes widened imperceptibly as her message scored home. Even though the soldier pressed harder and the blood quickened, flowing down his neck, Obadiah continued, "I *believe* you are mistaken. This old woman is *crazy* about babies because she never could have a child." He looked desperately into her eyes, hoping he had received the right message and apologizing for his painful words. Immediately, she confirmed his words; when she said, "Babies," the next time, she let a little spittle fly and started drooling from the

---

[8]   Exodus 1:15–20.

[9]   1 Samuel 21:13.

side of her mouth. The story of David reverberated through her mind as she thought of him in the hostile Philistine camp pretending to be crazy with spittle running down his beard as he scratched on wooden doors.

"Babies? I love babies," she explained, wild-eyed. "Do you have a baby? Please give me a baby. I want a baby." She crooned. She rocked an imaginary baby and then crooked her fingers at the legionnaire. "Can I hold your baby? I want your baby."

One of the legionnaires laughed nervously. Although he could cold-bloodedly run his sword through any person with no remorse, dealing with lunatics always made him nervous.

"Did you hear that, Tertius? She wants to have your baby. Are you going to give her a baby?" he said, mocking his leader.

Tertius yelled, "Shut up!" and said, "Before I killed that lady's baby, she told me this was the lady who came to birth all the babies."

Obadiah bravely spoke up. "Your Aramaic is good but rusty. If you asked for the woman who comes to birth all babies, she may have thought you were asking for the woman who comes to all the babies' births. Since my wife could never have a baby, she loves to go to every birth of a new baby. She loves to hold new babies."

On cue, Rachel said, "Do you have a new baby?" As she plucked at his arm with her fingernails, she asked, "Can I hold your baby?"

The tense interrogation scene shifted into one of mocking laughter as the other soldiers laughed at their leader's predicament. In frustration, he punched Obadiah in the face with his left hand and swung his sword at Rachel's head. She resignedly held her head high, knowing that at least the baby was safe as the side of her head exploded in pain. Dimly, she was aware of the soldiers leaving and Obadiah holding her in his lap.

As she slowly came to, she heard wails and heartbroken sobs coming from the village. She realized she was alive. At the last instant, the soldier must have turned his sword and struck her with the flat of his blade.

"Did they kill all the babies?" she asked imploringly of Obadiah, hoping that he would deny the anguished shrieks and screams she had heard before being struck down.

"I'm sorry," he whispered, and he held her tight as she sobbed, naming each one in her mind that she had delivered over the past two years. "All the baby boys," he whispered. "But the soldiers are leaving. They are returning to Jerusalem. No one gave away the location of anyone else's baby, even though beaten or offered the false hope of saving their own child. He is safe."

"Will we ever see him again?" she wondered aloud.

"Whether we see him again or not, we know our deliverance is near and that we have been blessed to have seen and held him," he gently reminded her.

"I will miss him," she said sadly. "But now I must go comfort those who are here."

She ignored his protests and her aching head as he helped her up. She gathered up her bandages and supplies to go outside to provide what aid she could. She knew most of the wounds were invisible, hearts slashed apart by the murders of the sons, and too deep for her salve to heal. But she held on fiercely to the hope for her nation within her. "The Deliverer will come." She knew that she had delivered her Deliverer. Faithfully, she had fulfilled her part in protecting her Redeemer, who would save the nation. Although it seemed impossible that this tiny baby was their promised Savior, she repeated to herself what Mary had often told her: "For nothing is impossible with God."

★   ★   ★